Madam Spry

and the

Secret Plans

Joy Cowley

Signatures
Madam Spry and the Secret Plans

This edition published by
Clean Slate Press Ltd.
9 George St, Mt Eden
Auckland 1024, New Zealand
www.cleanslatepress.com

Author: Joy Cowley
Designed by: McGraw-Hill Australia Pty Ltd.
Illustrations by: Gaston Vanzet

Text © Joy Cowley
Design and illustrations © McGraw-Hill Australia Pty Ltd. 2007
This edition published by Clean Slate Press Ltd. with the permission
of McGraw-Hill Australia Pty Ltd.
Originally published by McGraw-Hill Australia Pty Ltd. 2007

© This edition 2008 Clean Slate Press Ltd.

23 22 21 20 19 18 17 16
12 11 10 9 8 7 6 5 4 3

ISBN: 978-1-877454-35-6

Printed in China

RENFREWSHIRE COUNCIL	
242016821	
Bertrams	03/05/2017
	£4.99
BOW	

Contents

1 Top secret

Madam Spry, the very sly spy, had a parcel in the mail. "Look, Hugo," she said to her large, shaggy dog. "This will be the new chopper cap I ordered from Spy Products."

Hugo yawned and nudged his empty food bowl.

Madam Spry unwrapped the new cap with its tiny motor and fine silver blades. "I ordered it in red leather to match my spy suit. Isn't it beautiful? It's powerful, too. When I put this cap on my head and switch it on, it will lift me high off the ground. Very useful for tall fences and busy streets! They say the motor's so quiet you can hardly hear it."

Hugo put a large paw in the food bowl and whined softly.

1

"Sorry, Hugo. I forgot. You need more dog biscuits." She got up and fetched the bag from the cupboard.

But biscuits were not what Hugo wanted. He had his heart set on a large, juicy steak. As the dry biscuits rattled into his bowl, he turned his back on them and lay down with his head on his paws.

"I know I promised you steak," she said, "but we can't afford it. When we do the next job, you'll get steak—I promise."

Hugo sighed. He had heard these promises many times before.

Madam Spry went through the rest of the mail. "Hugo, this looks interesting. It's a letter from the Department of Defence and it's labelled TOP SECRET." She tore open the envelope and unfolded a crisp sheet of blank paper. "Ah, a message in invisible ink. Pass me my spyglass, Hugo."

Hugo got up, walked to the table, took the spyglass in his mouth and dropped it in Madam Spry's lap.

She wiped off the spit and held the glass over the paper. "How exciting! The Minister of Defence wants an urgent meeting with me.

That means he needs my help!" The very thought was too much for her. She burst into song, even though she knew that her voice cracked windows and blew up toasters.

My name is Madam Violet Spry
and I'm a global super spy.
Very smart and very sly,
with my chopper hat I fly ...

She paused to think of some more lines, and noticed that a leg had fallen off the table.

"Bother," she said.

Hugo put his head back and howled.

"Yes, Hugo, I know it's my voice. It's the price I have to pay for being a powerful woman."

Hugo rolled his eyes. Very slowly he walked to the food bowl and crunched on a dry doggy biscuit.

2 Secrets and rewards

The Minister of Defence had pink cheeks and a bow tie to match. He took Violet Spry into the interview room and pointed to a soft leather chair. "Thank you for coming, Madam Spry. Your country has need of you."

Madam Spry sat on the edge of her chair. "It does? Why?"

The minister folded his fine pink hands across his middle. "Have you heard of Walter J Honeymaker?"

"Is he the billionaire?" she asked.

"Billions and billions," replied the minister. "But the man himself is a mystery. I'm afraid the government is very suspicious of Walter J Honeymaker."

"Really?"

"We have reason to believe he is not a loyal citizen."

Madam Spry frowned. "Why? What has he done?"

The minister got up from his chair and whispered in her ear, "Walter J Honeymaker is friendly with every country in the world. That means he cannot be loyal to his own people."

"Oh." Madam Spry thought about this idea. "I see."

"He is also building a very large factory in Greenland. No one knows what the factory is for. It's so closely guarded we can't get near it. But we think it's being built for a super-duper mega-bomb."

Violet Spry gasped and clutched her throat. "Oh, no!"

"Oh, yes!" replied the minister. "At this moment, Walter J Honeymaker is in his yacht moored in the harbour. We picked up a phone message he left for his wife. Listen!" He pressed a button on a tape-recorder. There was a crackling noise, then a man's voice. "Sweetheart, I'm going to conquer the world. Do you hear? I'm going to have the whole wide world in the palm of my hand!"

Madam Spry shivered. "He's crazy!" she exclaimed.

"Dangerously so," said the minister. "I told you that we can't get near his factory in Greenland. But we do know he has the factory plans on board his yacht. Madam Spry, we need you to get a copy of those plans for us."

Her heart skipped a beat with the thrill of danger and adventure. "I'll do it!" she said.

The minister put his hand on hers, "I knew we could count on you, Madam Spry. Believe me, you will be well rewarded."

She thought about this too. "I get the reward afterwards?"

He nodded.

"If I get back alive," she added.

He smiled. "Of course. Remember, Madam Spry, you are doing this for your country. Isn't that the greatest reward anyone could wish for?"

❸ *Plans and gadgets*

Madam Spry knew it was safe to tell her dog of the top-secret mission. Hugo wouldn't tell a soul. But he was a very brave dog, and when she mentioned danger, he jumped up and down and wagged his tail.

"I'm sorry, Hugo. You can't come. This is something I must do on my own," said Madam Spry bravely.

He lay down with his head on his paws and whimpered.

"But I promise you," she said, "when I come back with the plans, you will have steak every night for a week."

Hugo gave his heard-it-before sigh and went to sleep. Belonging to a world-famous spy was not easy.

Madam Spry, on the other hand, was wide awake and busy. She studied photos of Walter J Honeymaker with his grandchildren. The pictures were proof that dangerous men could look as nice as Santa Claus. She also went over the design of his big private yacht so she would know how to get on board without alarming the crew. She would have to cross the harbour in silence. But any boat with motor or oars—

Her thoughts stopped right there. She was an excellent gymnast. She could do 500 push-ups and walk like a fly down the wall of a high building. But she had never been able to swim more than the width of the school pool.

"What will I do, Hugo? All that water ..."

Hugo opened his eyes and slowly got to his feet. He picked up the chopper cap and put it in her lap.

"I can't fly, Hugo. They will see me on the yacht's radar."

Hugo sighed, stood on his hind legs, reached up to the bench and knocked over a packet of plastic drinking straws.

His mistress laughed. "Well done, Hugo. But maybe I'll find something bigger than a drinking straw."

That night, Madam Spry, the very sly spy, put on her red leather spy suit with thirteen pockets and her fly-foot boots. She tucked her hair under the shiny red cap and pushed open her window. "Wish me luck, Hugo," she said, as she stepped outside.

Nimbly Madam Spry walked down the wall of her apartment building, her feet sucking onto the concrete. The streets were empty and no one saw her. Which was a pity, she thought. It was quite exciting when people looked up and screamed.

Two blocks away was the harbour, with ships nestled against a wharf. As silent as a shadow, Madam Spry slipped past the night-watchmen and scurried down steps wet with the sea. Here in the dark, she adjusted the strap on her chopper cap, pulled down her goggles and switched on the chopper motor. The propeller whirled like a whining mosquito. Good, she thought. The noise would not be heard. Madam Spry took a length of plastic tubing from a leg pocket and put it in her mouth. Then she checked her luminous wrist compass. All was ready. It was time to go.

④ *Mission accomplished?*

The sea was dark and cold, but a brave spy could not make a fuss. "My country needs me," she said to herself through the tube, as she put her head in the water.

The chopper hat worked very well, exactly like an outboard motor in reverse. The vibration made her head itch, but she couldn't do anything about that. She sped through the water, breathing through the tube and checking her compass.

Through her goggles, Madam Spry saw silver fish shapes in the water. She wondered if there were any sharks around. Were sharks attracted to red leather? She was relieved when the beacon on her compass told her that the yacht was very close.

She lifted her head out of the water. The yacht was huge and strung with rows of coloured lights. She would have to be very careful or someone would see her.

Holding on to the anchor chain, Madam Spry tucked her breathing tube back in place and pulled a length of spider wire from another pocket. With a flick of her wrist, she wound the wire around the bollard on the bow. Then, hand over hand, she climbed up until she was standing dripping on the deck.

This, Madam Spry knew, was her most dangerous mission yet.

Some of the crew were still up; she could hear them talking. She moved from shadow to shadow until she came to that part of the yacht with the main cabin. She could see a light in a porthole. A big man with bushy white eyebrows was sitting at a desk, playing card games on his computer. Beside him was a roll of paper that could be sea charts—or the plans of a bomb factory!

Madam Spry had to wait until Walter J Honeymaker was tired enough to shut down his computer, put out the light and go into his sleeping quarters. When all was quiet, she went inside. From one of her pockets she pulled out a spyglass with a built-in laser light. Her heart beat fast as she unrolled those papers on the desk. Yes, yes! These were the plans of the factory!

She took off her watch—which was also a phone, television and camera—and held it to her eye. She bent over the desk and clicked. A small spurt of water landed plop, on the plans.

Oh stinkypoo! The watch camera was full of water! Ruined!

From yet another pocket she took a waterproof plastic bag. No one stirred as she stuffed in the plans, then tucked the bag inside her spy suit. Another minute and she was outside, climbing down the spider wire and into the sea.

Mission accomplished! she thought.

Well, not quite accomplished.

Madam Spry had forgotten that leather did not like to be soaked in sea water. Neither did the chopper motor. The propeller turned for a while, then got slower. Water gurgled in her ears and the spy suit grew soggy and heavy. Then the motor stopped and there was no sound except for the sea.

Still breathing through the tube, Violet Spry looked at her compass. She was far from the shore and she couldn't swim. What would she do?

Your country needs you, she said to herself. You have to deliver this plastic bag with the secret plans.

She tried kicking but she didn't seem to move far. A crowd of small silver fish came into the light of her compass and stared at her with round eyes. Then they all rushed away, as though frightened of something. Madam Spry was trying not to think "Shark, shark", when something grabbed her arm in its jaws.

She screamed and her mouth filled with water.

It wasn't a shark. Faithful hound Hugo had come to meet her and help her home.

5 Mission failed

Madam Spry had a slight head cold. Her chopper cap and red leather spy suit were ruined and so was her multi-purpose spy watch. But that didn't matter. Any moment, the Minister of Defence would bring her a reward for the plans and her bravery.

"Steak for a week, Hugo," she promised.

But she didn't hear from the minister, and when she phoned his office, he was busy. Two days passed and Madam Spry visited the Department of Defence.

"I need to see the minister at once, or else," she demanded.

"Or else what?" asked the woman at the front desk.

"Or I'll sing a song," replied Madam Spry.

14

The woman shuddered. The last time Madam Spry had sung in the building, smoke had come out of the computers. "I'll see what I can do," she said.

Today, the Minister of Defence did not offer the nice soft leather chair. He told Madam Spry quite bluntly that her mission had failed.

"But I got you the plans," she said.

"Yes, you brought in some plans," he replied.

"They were for Walter J Honeymaker's factory in Greenland." she insisted.

"Indeed they were," said the minister, with the faintest smile. "Do you know what it is? An ice-cream factory!"

"Ice-cream?" She stared at his round pink face. "Mr Minister, you said it was a factory for super-duper mega-bombs!"

The minister scratched his ear. "Come now, Madam Spry. I'm sure you misheard me. We have returned the plans, of course. Mr Honeymaker was very upset. The factory is secret because it's for a delicious new ice-cream that has no fat, no sugar and not a single kilojoule."

"But you played me a tape. He said he was going to conquer the world!"

"Madam, you did not hear a tape in this room. If Mr Honeymaker talked about having the world in the palm of his hand, I'm sure he was referring to the ice-cream market."

Madam Spry took a deep breath. "What about my reward?

"Reward?" The Minister of Defence laughed. "Madam Spry, you stole those plans from Mr Honeymaker's yacht and we have returned them. Let's just call it quits. Now, if you'll excuse me, I'm busy."

Madam Spry wanted to screech a song right there in his room, but she didn't. She spun on her heel and stormed out of the Department of Defence. Madam Spry wondered what she was going to tell poor Hugo, who was at home, waiting for his steak.

On the front steps of the building, stood some young reporters with cameras. "Madam Spry! A moment, please! We heard a rumour that you've been working for the Department of Defence?"

"I don't want to talk about it," she said, trying to walk past them.

One young woman stepped in front of her. "Does this have anything to do with Walter J Honeymaker and his bomb factory?"

"It's not a bomb factory," she said, "it's an ice-cream factory." Then, before she knew it, she was telling them everything.

That night, the story was on every radio and TV news station. The next morning, the papers had headlines like MEGA WEAPON IS ZERO KILOJOULE ICE-CREAM. It became the biggest joke of the year. Mr Honeymaker was interviewed by TV reporters from all over the world. The Minister of Defence, however, went on holiday and was not available for comment.

"He's embarrassed, and so he should be," said Madam Spry, pouring dog biscuits into Hugo's dish. "Never mind, Hugo. Next job, you get steak, I promise you."

6 Unexpected success

Madam Spry did not get many visitors, so when there was a thunderous knocking at her door, she thought it was the landlord complaining because she had not yet paid her rent.

She opened the door a few centimeters. The big man in front of her was none other than Walter J Honeymaker. Oh-oh, she thought. He's come to have me arrested for stealing his secret plans.

The man put out his hand. "Madam Spry? I'm Walter J Honeymaker and I've been busy as a bee trying to find you to thank you."

"Thank me?" She shook her head, imagining she still had water in her ears.

"Why yes, Madam Spry. I know what

happened. I kept my factory so secret that the government thought I was up to no good. But I tell you, my ice-cream is going to make the world a better place." His bushy eyebrows wiggled. "Madam Spry, I had only one problem. I didn't know how I was going to advertise this ice-cream worldwide. But you did that for me, Madam Spry. Now everyone knows about Honeymaker ice-cream and we've gone into production early. I couldn't buy the kind of publicity you got me." He took something from his pocket. "I've come here to thank you with a nice big cheque."

Madam Spry took the cheque, looked at it and fainted clean away.

Her faint did not last long. By evening she had paid the landlord, ordered a new red leather spy suit, chopper cap and multi-purpose spy watch, and taken Hugo down to the supermarket to buy a shopping bag full of the best steak.

That night she had smoked salmon, grapes, green jelly beans and a strawberry milkshake for her supper. "Hugo," she cried, "I'm so happy! I feel a little song coming on." She stood up.

Hugo cast a worried look at the toaster, the stove and the window.

She threw out her arms and took a deep breath.

I'm Madam Spry,
a very clever spy—oomph!

The "oomph" came when Hugo pushed a large raw steak into her mouth.

From the author

I grew up with stories of super-heroes, men who did brave deeds, were always good and never made mistakes. To be honest, they were quite boring. As a change, I thought it would be fun to have a woman spy who was not very brave or smart, who was rather conceited, and who would have made a lot of mistakes without a clever dog to keep an eye on her. So that's how we have Madam Spry in her red leather spy suit with thirteen pockets, her fly-foot boots that walk up walls, and her patient dog Hugo.

The Department of Defence need a super-spy to find out why Walter J Honeymaker is building a huge factory in Iceland. Violet Spry is the woman for the job. With her chopper hat and snorkel she can travel underwater to the billionaire's yacht, where the secret plans are stored.

The job should be easy, but the life of a spy is full of surprises and enemies are not always easy to identify.

Joy Cowley

21

From the illustrator

I had a great time illustrating the Madam Spry books. When I like the stories I illustrate, the pictures always seem to come out better and are easier to draw.

Each story is full of great images so the images for the covers and chapter headings were easy to choose. The stories are like fast-moving cartoons or adventure movies ... one minute we are down in the deep sea, then we are climbing the sides of high-rise buildings, being caught in traps, dealing with fiendish villains, making lucky escapes—and more.

Being the illustrator, I was with Madam Violet Spry, the very sly spy, every step of the way. How lucky can you get.

Have fun with Madam Spry. I did.

Gaston Vanzet